I Want Your Moo

A Story for Children About Self-Esteem

Published by
MAGINATION PRESS
An Educational Publishing Foundation Book
American Psychological Association
750 First Street, NE
Washington, DC 20002

Book design by Sandra Kimbell
Printed by Worzalla, Stevens Point, Wisconsin

Library of Congress Cataloging-in-Publication Data
Weiner, Marcella Bakur
  I want your moo : a story for children about self-esteem / by Marcella Bakur Weiner and Jill Neimark ; illustrated by JoAnn Adinolfi.
  p. cm.
  "An Educational Publishing Foundation Book."
  Summary: Disliking her appearance and the gobbling noise she makes, Toodles the Turkey tries to persuade
  other animals to give her their sounds.
  ISBN-13: 978-1-4338-0542-4 (hardcover : alk. paper)
  ISBN-10: 1-4338-0542-1 (hardcover : alk. paper)
  ISBN-13: 978-1-4338-0552-3 (pbk. : alk. paper)
  ISBN-10: 1-4338-0552-9 (pbk. : alk. paper) [1. Self-esteem—Fiction. 2. Animal sounds—Fiction. 3. Turkeys—Fiction. 4. Animals—Fiction.]
  I. Neimark, Jill. II. Adinolfi, JoAnn, ill. III. Title.
PZ7.W436366lab 2010
[E]--dc22
2009004560

10 9 8 7 6 5 4 3 2 1

First Printing September 2009

J
E
WEI

K-3
(200)

I Want Your Moo

A Story for Children
About Self-Esteem

Second Edition

Marcella Bakur Weiner, EdD, PhD
and Jill Neimark

illustrated by
JoAnn Adinolfi

Magination Press • Washington, DC
American Psychological Association

Toodles the Turkey did not like herself.

Her legs were like sticks.

Her head had no hair.

Her feathers were brown.

But most of all, Toodles hated her sound.

Gobble-gobble. Gobble-gobble.

What a horrible noise!

I can't stand the sound of my voice.

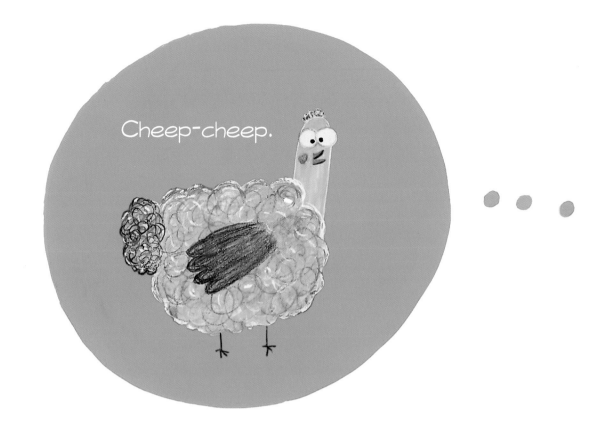

When she was a baby chick, Toodles was soft and fuzzy. And her sound was soft and fuzzy. Cheep-cheep. But when she learned to talk like the other turkeys, her Cheep-cheep turned into

Gobble-gobble.

One day, Toodles could stand her Gobble-gobble no longer. She wanted a new sound.

"I want your Moo," Toodles begged Cathy the Cow. "It's long and it's strong and I want it!"

Cathy moved her head slowly. She chomped some grass. She said, "You can't have my Moo. It's part of me!"

Mooo-oooo-oo-

Toodles went to Paris the Pig. "Will you give me your Oink? It's so smart and so tough."

Paris rolled in the mud and wiggled his snout. "No, you can't have my Oink. You're not a pig."

Oink!

Toodles went to Harry the Horse. "Your Neigh is so gentle. Can I please have your Neigh just for the day?"

"No Neigh, I'm sorry to say," said Harry as he munched on some hay.

She asked the duck for his Quack,
the goose for his Clack,

the crow for her Caa-aaw,
and the cat for her Mee-oow.

And they all said, "NO WAY!"

Doodle-doo,

Toodles went to Ralph the Rooster. "I love your Cocka-doodle-doo. Each morning you sing it loud and wake up the world."

Ralph stretched his neck to the sky proudly. "I can't give you all of my sound."

Toodles sighed in disappointment. "Well, even a tiny piece would be nice," said Toodles.

"Okay," said Ralph kindly. "I'll give you the Doodle-doo and I'll keep the rest. Is it a deal?"

Toodles couldn't believe her luck.

doodle-doo, doodle-doo

she cried,
spinning around.

The next morning, just before dawn, when the world was still dark, Toodles was fast asleep. Ralph ran over and shook her. "Wake up! The sun is almost up! We have to sing to let everyone know morning is here!"

The sun was rising over the field. Toodles grumbled and rubbed her eyes.

Doodle-doo, doodle-doo.

"Wait," said Ralph. "Let's sing together. One—two—three—sing!"

Cocka-cocka! Doodle!

Doodle-cocka-doodle! Doodle!

Cocka-cocka-do!

Doo-doo-doo-doo-doo!

Ralph looked at Toodles. And Toodles looked at Ralph. It wasn't working. The whole barnyard was still asleep. Toodles made one last Doodle-doo and ran away.

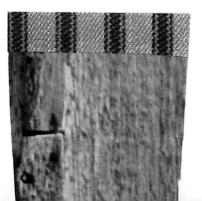

Toodles gobbled sadly, sitting under a tree.
Far above, Omar the Owl heard.

"Whoo-whoo," he called to Toodles.
"What's wrong?"

"I hate my Gobble-gobble!" cried Toodles.

Omar blinked his big eyes and said, "Once I wanted
a new sound, too. When I sang 'Whoo-whoo,'
everyone thought I was asking a question. They thought
I was dumb when really I am very wise."

"If I could have an Oink-oink or Bow-wow or Moo-moo or
Clack-clack, I'd be so glad I'd never look back," Toodles
moped. "Nobody's sound is as ugly as mine."

Omar flew down to Toodles and said, "Your sound is yours.
It is you. You have just the right sound, like I have
my Whoo."

But Toodles didn't believe it. She wandered away to the edge of the barnyard. The chicks were playing. "Cheep-cheep!" they laughed, running and falling and flapping their little wings. Toodles felt sad.

Then Toodles heard a loud, piercing sound.

Shreeeeek-shreek.

A shadow passed over the ground. The shadow moved in and got bigger. It was a hawk! All the chicks froze in fear.

Shreek-shreek! The hawk circled closer. His beak looked hard and mean. His huge wings flapped slowly. His sharp eyes looked down on his afternoon meal. Toodles moved fast and spread her wings around the chicks.

Gobble-gobble. Gobble-gobble!

said Toodles.

Gobblegobblegobble!

yelled Toodles. The hawk hesitated. Toodles flapped her wings and yelled again,

GOBBLEGOBBLEGOBBLE

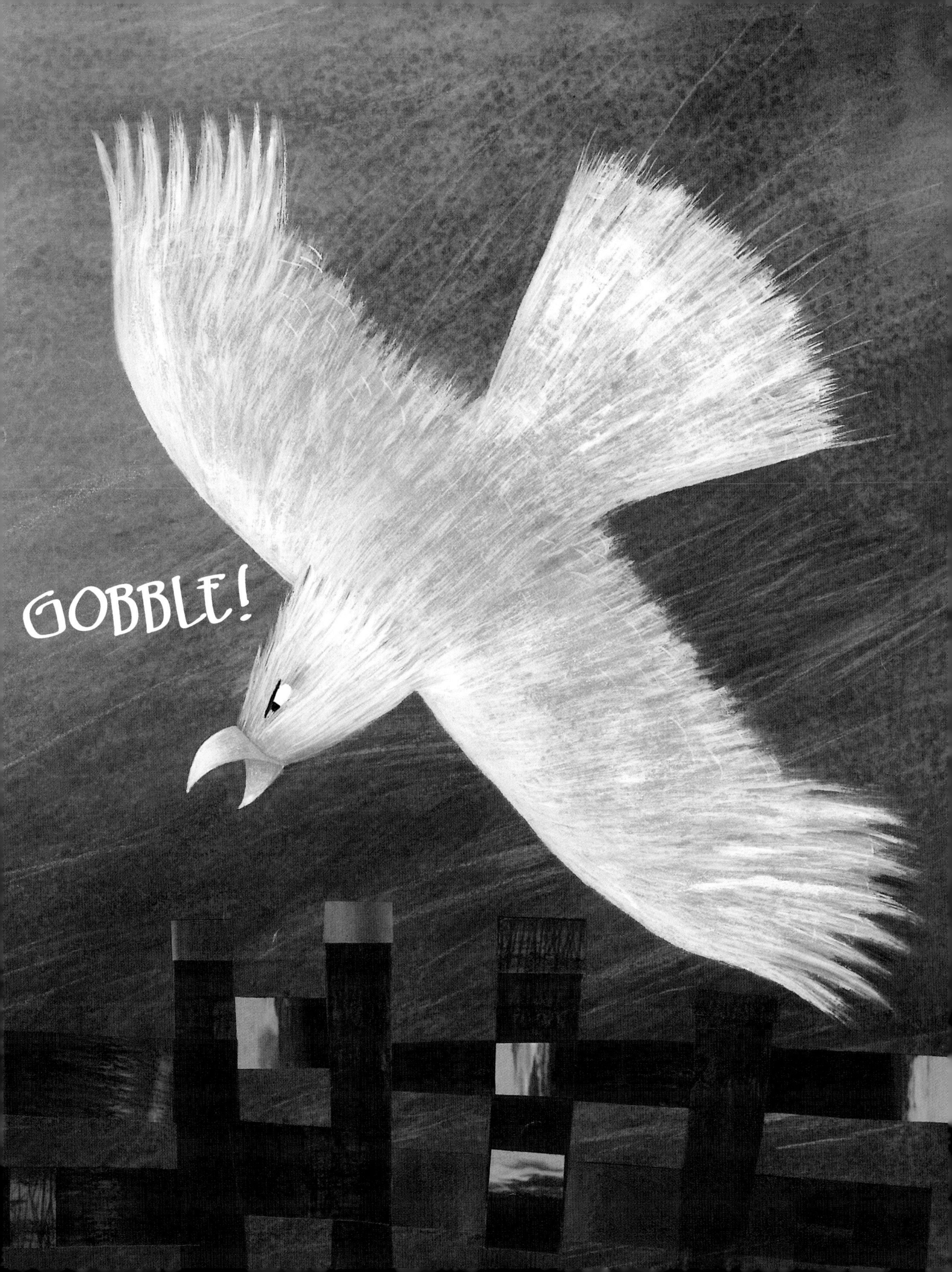
GOBBLE!

The hawk flew away!

Everyone cheered for Toodles. "Yay! Hooray for Toodles!"
The baby chicks ran in circles.

Toodles was so proud of herself.

"My legs are thin, so I can move fast. My feathers are like a warm, safe blanket. My sound is all mine. It's not ugly. It's all me!

Gobble-gobble-gobble.

I guess I'm the way I was always meant to be."

One of the greatest gifts we can give our children is helping them find a sense of self-worth. Children who lack this feeling often express it as "not liking" part of themselves as Toodles does in *I Want Your Moo*. Toodles despises the sound of her Gobble-gobble. And just like many children, she is expressing her overwhelming lack of confidence and comfort with herself. But her self-esteem is restored with the eventual victory over self-doubt when she "saves the day" by using the very voice she so dislikes. If we can help foster our children's sense of their own unique value and worth, like Toodles they will be able to weather the inevitable challenges of life.

What is self-esteem?

Self-esteem is built upon self-concept. When you perceive that many qualities about yourself are positive, then you have high self-esteem. If a child, for instance, feels positive about his physical appearance, accomplishments, and capabilities, his self-esteem is good. The more positive these feelings, the higher his self-esteem.

Children who lack self-esteem are unhappy with their own self-concept, essentially the *who, what,* and *how* that they are. Their low self-esteem might reveal itself in feelings of sadness, anger, or fear. Kids might not be aware of the connection between their emotions and actions and their low self-esteem. For some children, pulling away from friends and family, having an inability to concentrate, or being critical of everyone and everything is their expression of this gnawing hurt. Other kids may express low self-esteem as not liking a particular part of themselves through questions or statements, such as "Why are my ears so big?" or "I hate my hair." Other children may not feel capable compared to others. This is often expressed as fear or anxiety, such as not wanting to try out for a sports team, saying, "I'm too short. I'll never make it. Everyone is bigger than me." Or a child might say, "I just don't want to go to the party. I won't know anyone. I want to stay home." She does not even want to try to make new friends, determined that she will

eventually be rejected by them. Or a child might argue endlessly with his sister, convinced that his parents certainly favor her over him anyway.

What can parents do to "build" self-esteem?

Listen to your children. First and foremost, before taking any action, parents must listen to their children. Listening is more than just hearing the words. It involves sensing the emotion behind the words and also intuiting unspoken words. If a child says, "I didn't make the team. They didn't want me," you might then say, "You tried your very best. I am sure the coach was impressed with your sportsmanship and good hustle. Maybe with a little more practice with ball handling you'll be an excellent addition to the team next year. If you'd like, I will help you." Also, read between the lines of what your child is saying. If your child tells you that his best friend was chosen for the school play but he doesn't really care that he didn't make the cast, you might ask him, "Maybe Eli can practice his lines with you, if he's up for that. This may help your feelings, and give you a chance to participate in the play. And it would be fun to rehearse with Eli, don't you think?" Additionally, this would help mitigate his feelings of jealousy and might create a stronger friendship between the two friends.

Encourage children to explore their emotions. A child may not be able to tell you exactly what he feels. Sometimes the best way to know is to observe how he acts. Children act out their experiences. The child who starts hitting others, who no longer wants to go to school, or who is having nightmares is feeling all kinds of emotions, particularly anger and fear. A child who is overcome by sadness may be withdrawn or apathetic. He may suddenly shrug off activities that have excited him in the past and be quick to tears. What you can do is help your child label the emotion directly without judgment: "Are you angry because your racing game is difficult? Maybe that is why you hit Theo, because you are frustrated. With some practice and patience, I know you can do it and I can help you if you would like." And, end it with a hug and kisses (or your signs of love and acceptance). Your child's budding self-esteem is further nourished by his ability to live out his emotions safely and not worrying how you may judge him for having those feelings.

Emphasize your child's unique self. Parents can help children develop self-esteem by providing them with opportunities to develop interests and hobbies, and in turn feel good about themselves. With his parents' support, a child can explore and discover himself and his own unique personality and talents. For one child, it will be playing the piano; for another, it might be participating in soccer; and for a third, it could be learning math. And yet another's great talent may be charisma and people skills.

Whatever it is, parents should observe and be sensitive to their child's experience, and allow the child to choose the activities. Well-meaning parents can make mistakes by channeling a child's activities in the way they think is best. Watch what your child loves to do and then follow that by providing him with more of what he is enjoying. If your daughter sighs and whines each time she has to practice the piano, then you know that this is not an activity for her. If your son is pushed to play sport but would rather draw and paint, you can encourage him to express himself and give positive feedback that supports and encourages his interests. In this way, not only will his talents blossom, but so will his self-concept and self-love. It is here that the sense of identity is established and recognition of his uniqueness is found.

Help buffer a temporary loss of self-esteem. While parents cannot control a specific, temporary loss of self-esteem, they can quickly repair the effects. For example, if your daughter was not invited to a sleepover at a friend's house, you might offer her another activity which you could all enjoy, such as a picnic or a day trip. Or you could ask her if she would like to have another friend over. You might say, "I know you're disappointed and it is difficult that things didn't work out with Lela's sleepover. How about we see if Abby is free tomorrow for a playdate or a movie?" Or if she didn't make the choir this year,

you might say, "I am proud of you and think you are courageous for trying out for choir. I love your enthusiasm, effort, and everything about you, too!" This can restore her original feeling of self-worth by helping her learn to overcome disappointment.

Create a sense of belonging. Encouraging a sense of belonging to certain demographic or cultural groups might help children boost their self-esteem and instill a sense of pride and self-worth. A child realizes, for instance, "I am an 8-year-old, brown-eyed, Catholic African-American girl with four brothers and sisters." This characterization may help a child accept and love who she is. She can be told of grandparents and great grandparents, of her connection to other countries from which her ancestors emigrated, and of her ancestors' accomplishments and struggles. You can teach family traditions and introduce your child to other customs by taking her to church, synagogue, or mosque.

Celebrate individuality. Just as no two persons have the same fingerprints, no two children, not even those in the same family, are the same. Even identical twins are different. Nonetheless, a sense of self comes about by looking at others in order to determine and define who we are as individuals. As we discover that our qualities have an absolute character, we learn that we are a unique blend that represents us alone. As parents and teachers, we can help children value their own individuality, and thus teach them to not compare themselves entirely with their friends and siblings or judge their own worth based upon another person's qualities.

Parents can also learn to know their children inside-out. And no matter what your child does or says or how he behaves, he should know clearly and strongly that he is loved for who he is. Teach him that he can depend on that—today, tomorrow, and forever.

You are, in all likelihood, the best resource for helping your child find ways to build self-esteem and develop a sense of self-worth. However, if you find that your child's distress persists or interferes with daily activities, we recommend consulting a child psychologist for further guidance.